Round II

KinFolk

Round II

Belle Publishing LLC Oklahoma City, Ok 73107
www.bellepublishingllc.co
bellepublishingllc@gmail.com
First Edition
ISBN- 978-1-7349541-6-6

First off, I want to thank my Team Belle Publishing LLC for continuing to give authors like me a chance to write.

The models Shemika T, Jai, Tyler S, and MoneyMan. Thank you for the way you blessed Round II. Together you guys made history with this beautiful cover.

To the one who always snaps for KinFolk, she always shows up and shows out just because she can and we love it; Sunee Rice of Rice Photography OKC, thank you for everything.

Kenyetta, you continue to put in work not only for me but for every person you encounter. I'm a true witness to your dedication and I'm proud to be a part of this journey.

Finally, My wife who has been patient with every line I write even though I am the most difficult client. I thank you for taking your time with me and the inspiration you put in this book. It was fun coming up with this one. I love you.

And now, Let's get Freaky.

1

Winter

"Bruh, I'm glad I left Tina at the house cause the club is popping tonight," Mali said as he took a sip of Hennessey.

"Dogg, why you even get married when you could have been like me and just stayed a freak but naw, your ass wanna *believe in love*," Peanut said tapping his shoulders.

"Hold on Peanut don't get it twisted Dogg, I love Tina and she's a great wife but sometimes I just wanna fuck and feel something different," Mali said.

"Mane what the fuck you talking bout, cause niggas get married to only be with one while other niggas stay single to fuck em all," Peanut asked laughing loud.

"I feel you but honestly I get tired of the *same ol same ol* and tonight I want some *New New,* so you got my back wit, Tina, right?" Mali said.

"As always Dogg, so who you checking out in here tonight with all these choices." Peanut said

"Naw, Dogg, I got this sexy lil thick thang I hit up on Facebook that's cool as hell, so I'm about to send her a message and see what's up," Mali said.

"Pulling my move, I see. Well, do your thang, Dogg, I'm on the dance floor," Peanut said.

"Aight, Dogg, I'll get at you in a minute," Mali said, showing love.

"Bet." Peanut went to the dance floor then turned towards the bar. He pulled out his phone and started texting.

Peanut: Hey baby. What you doing?

Baby: Hey Daddy. Nothing just watching tv. Wyd?

Peanut: I'm at the club with a few of da homies. Chilling.

Baby: Chilling? So…what time you plan on coming home?

Peanut: Don't start asking questions. When I get there.

5

He put his phone back in his pocket and when he looked up, Mali was walking towards him.

"Yo Dogg I'm bout to ride out and see what's up with shorty. I'll hit you in the morning." Mali said as they showed love.

Mali walked out the club as Peanut went back to the dance floor when he turned around and saw Tina looking sexy as fuck.

"Damn, Tina you looking good in the club tonight," he said grabbing her waist.

"Well thank you Peanut," Tina said.

"I thought you were at home tonight?" Peanut asked.

"I was then I got bored so when life 360 told me Mali left the club I came in; so now can I get a drink?" Tina asked with a smile.

"Since you bad as fuck, I'm gonna go get you that drink. What you want?" Peanut asked.

"Hennessey margarita," Tina said as she rubbed her ass on Peanut.

Damn, this the homie wife with this nice ass making my dick hard as fuck. He thought as he turned her around.

"So, you trying to have some Wintertime sex tonight"? He said. Tina looked at Peanut with a shocking face. "Peanut now you know I'm married," Tina said. He pulled her close to him looking into her eyes.

"Not for the next hour, right?" Peanut said with a sneaky look on his face as he grabbed her ass. "I guess not," Tina said.

"Come on ain't no one gonna know so meet me outside," Peanut said. He turned and walked towards the door.

Tina stood there thinking about how much she wanted to fuck someone other than Mali and how she wanted to feel passion and pleasure. Her thoughts got so deep she started touching herself in the club. "Fuck, niggas ain't shit," She said to herself. She walked to the door and opened it as Peanut was waiting by her car.

"Your ass didn't even buy my drink," she said. Peanut laughed as he opened her door. "That's because I don't wanna taste Hennessey while I'm eating that pussy tonight. "She smiled as he closed her door. He got in on the passenger side.

"Let's go to that hotel down the street," Peanut said.

"Okay," Tina responded as she put the car in drive.

They made it to the hotel in five minutes. The cold winter air came through the car as Peanut got out to go pay for the room.

Tina felt nervous and guilty but knew it was time to do something for herself even if it was getting herself in trouble, so she silenced her phone as Peanut got back in the car.

"Room 102," he said pointing as she put the car in drive.

"Peanut, what your girl think about you fucking other bitches?" Tina asked. Peanut gave her a look before he spoke.

"My social media say SINGLE everywhere so I can fuck who I want when I want which is why I stay single."

She parked the car and they got out in the thick cold of the winter air as the chills went through her body and she knew it was about to go down. Peanut opened the door and walked in as she followed. She walked in thinking to herself. *He didn't even let me go first but whatever, I just need some dick.*

He got on the bed and lay on a pillow then grabbed the remote. "Come lay next to me," he said as he turned the channels. Tina took off her shoes and got in bed with the first man other than her husband since she had been married. Peanut felt her nervousness, so he got up and grabbed a blunt from his coat.

"What's up, you wanna smoke a little bit? May help you relax," he said lighting the blunt. "Yeah, I will hit it a few times," she said as he handed her the blunt.

"Damn," he said as she hit the blunt.

"You said I could hit the blunt," she said looking confused.

"I know I just love the way your lips look around that blunt," he said smiling. She giggled as she reached to hand him the blunt.

"Naw hold on to that," he said as he crawled in bed. He started kissing her neck and felt her body relax so he moved his hands exploring her body continuing to kiss different parts of her neck. He grabbed the blunt as he raised her shirt and took it off revealing her beautiful skin.

He threw the shirt and continued kissing her stomach using his tongue to play with her nipples as he unstrapped her bra and released the D's. She started moaning as he slowly licked her nipples while pinching the other as she pushed his head against her breasts.

She moaned feeling pleasure she hadn't felt in a while. It was like she was a virgin again as she pulled off his shirt. "That's nice Peanut, she said rubbing his chest, let me see some more."

She pulled off her pants and dropped them on the floor.

"Well shit, I guess I better catch up," Peanut said standing up. He unbuckled his belt and pants then let them fall to the floor but before he could take off his underwear she reached over and pulled them down.

"Okay, I see you," Tina said with a smile on her face looking at his dick. She thought to herself. Mali is this big soft before lying back in the bed. She looked at Peanut.

"Now come taste this pussy!"

"With pleasure," he said as he got on his knees and pulled her close to the edge of the bed. He started slow, licking the outside of her walls until her pussy was good and wet. She moaned and started grinding her hips.

He sat back and looked at the beauty in front of him before he took his tongue and split her pussy giving him access to her inner walls. She reached down and grabbed his head as she felt the pleasure of his tongue rotating inside her.

Damn this nigga's mouth feel good. Oh, Mali is going to kill me.

That thought made her cum again. Peanut threw her legs back and put his mouth on her clit giving it pleasure so good it made her cream all over his face. He sat back smiling as she laughed.

"Umm, sorry it's been a while since my pussy been ATE," she said smiling.

"No worries love. He said putting on a condom. He got on the bed and started kissing her body, paying attention to her face as he slid in. Her eyes opened like it was her first time feeling anything. She moaned as she wrapped her arms around Peanut.

His stroke was slow and steady making her feel all of him as he went deeper inside her. He raised her legs above her head and started giving her long strokes as he looked into her eyes. He could see she was being pleased. So, he continued.

"OH MY GOD!" she screamed as he thrusts his dick in and out of her. He was hitting it so good she bit his chest to keep from screaming. When she looked in his eyes, she enjoyed what she saw but feared it at the same time.

She grabbed his head and kissed him as he came hard and he fell on top of her. They both laughed as he rolled off her and got out the bed.

"Where you going?" she asked, giving him a look that said *what the fuck*.

"I'm going to take a shower. We been here 20 minutes, we gotta go," he said as he walked in the bathroom and closed the door.

"Damn, that seriously wasn't enough for me, I need a round two."

She got out of the bed and walked to the bathroom door, but it was locked. She laughed as she put on her clothes and left the room.

When she made it to the car, she thought to herself. *Was that worth it?* She pulled out her phone and seen there were no missed calls or texts.

"Guess that's my life," she said as she drove out the parking lot leaving Peanut at the hotel. "I really hate winter," she said as she drove home.

2

Spring

Mali was getting off work when his phone notification sounded. He looked and seen the text message from Andrea.

Andrea: Hey baby. How was your day?

Mali: Not too bad, about to finish it up at the gym. What you up to? How was your day?

Andrea: It was a long day. Fighting with my boyfriend all day. Now I'm about to get my nails done so I can feel better.

Mali: Damn, sorry to hear that baby, you wanna link up and have a drink?

Andrea: I don't need you teasing me today. Lol We been texting for months and I think I'm ready for a Spring Fling.

Mali: Lol. Teasing? Nah, Ma. I'm just being respectful. I'm married and you in a relationship so I'm not gonna rush you. You think you ready?

Andrea: Yes, I think I am. I sit and think about you even when I'm with him. I find myself sneaking and texting you while he's in the room. I daydream about how you will feel inside me.

Mali: Alright now, don't be catching no feelings on me.

Andrea: No feelings, at least I don't think so. I just wanna feel wanted and my man isn't doing it. Don't act like you don't be thinking about me when you with your wife?

Mali: I'm not gonna lie, you cross my mind a lot. Especially with those Snaps I get. What you doing tonight?

Andrea: IDK. Guess after I get my nails done, I will see how much money I have left to play with.

Mali: I tell you what, I'm gonna Cashapp you $100 to get your nails and toes done, you know I like them pretty feet, then just hit me if you can get out tonight.

Andrea: Awe, thank you, baby. You don't have to do that, I can pay for my own.

Maki: So, can I and I am. You wanna spend your money go buy yourself something cause I got that body.

Andrea: I hope so. Thank you. I will text you later. XOXO

Mali: Ok.

Mali went to his Cashapp and typed $200 then sent it to Andrea. He smiled.

After meeting Andrea on Messenger, they had been talking ever since wintertime. They had met up a few times, but he still hadn't hit it.

He thought as he walked into the gym.

Why am I waiting so long? I haven't even been with anyone else since I met her. I'm gonna have to see about tonight though. I want her bad, but Tina has been watching me close ever since that night I went to the club with Peanut. Crazy shit.

"PEANUT, what's good Bro?" Mali said walking to the weights.

"Trying to get it in Dogg what's good with you?" he said putting down the weights.

"Trying to burn some of this stress off hell, shit been tense at home," Mali said pulling out his gloves.

"Man, she still tripping about you going to the club?" Peanut said. He thought to himself. *I need to tell him. Not now though.*

"Hell yeah, over nothing though Dogg. I didn't even fuck that night. Shit, I haven't fucked since…hell I can't remember," Mali said lifting.

"You mean you ain't even fucking at home?" Peanut said picking up the Barbells.

"Nah, Dogg, we have sex, but it feels like obligation sex," Mali said as he was bench pressing.

"What the hell *is obligation sex*?" Peanut said laughing.

"Oh, I forgot you ain't in no relationship, Mali said laughing, it's simple."

"Well speak Dogg," Peanut said.

"Obligation sex is when you just fuck because that's what you have to do. You just wanna get it over with. The majority of the time it's just to shut someone up."

18

"OH, you mean like husbands do wives?" Peanut said interested.

"Like people do in any relationship Dogg," Mali said, "it's just like that."

"So, what's the good sex called?" Peanut asked.

"Passion, Dogg," Mali said getting off the bench, "Passion. When we both actually want each other, the sex is amazing. We just haven't wanted each other at the same time so it turns into an obligation."

"And that's when you hit Facebook," Peanut said laughing as his phone went off. He saw he had two texts.

"Yeah, you right." Mali laughed.

"You alright over there Dogg?"

"Yeah fam," Peanut said as he looked at the text from Tina asking to see him tonight. He looked at the other message from baby asking if they had plans tonight.

Fuck, he thought to himself.

"Well let's finish this workout," Mali said hitting his shoulder.

"Alright," Peanut said as he put his phone away.

They both continued their workout for the next hour. After they were done, Mali pulled out his phone and started taking pictures.

"Here we go with the story show," Peanut said laughing. "Niggas always posting gym pics."

"Man, don't hate me cause I'm 5'10 with pretty skin and a six-pack harder than an 82 Cadillac," Mali said snapping.

They both laughed as they left the locker room headed out the gym.

"What you about to get into Mali?" Peanut asked opening his car door.

"Shit, go to the crib and see what I did wrong today, smoke a few and lay It down," He responded? "What about you?"

"Man, I don't even know," Peanut said, "I guess go to the crib and see what's up for tonight."

"Bet hit me up," Mali said.

They both got in their whips and drove off. Peanut turned down the radio and called Tina. She answered fast.

"Hey, baby you know better than to call. What if Mali was here?" she answered.

"Calm down baby, I just left him plus we been fucking around for months and he ain't found out so I think we good," he said.

"Oh ok. So, what you doing," she said calming down. "I wanna see you tonight."

"Yeah, I know, I saw your text. I've got a few things to handle and I can get with you later. What time you gonna try and get out?" he said.

She sat on the couch before responding.

"I really don't have a set time but I do know he gonna come home with his attitude so he can close the door and talk to his side bitch all night."

"Girl please that nigga ain't fucking with nobody. He just got a lot on his mind," he said laughing. "Whatever you gonna lie for your homie," she said.

"I'm his homeboy fucking his wife so *apparently* I'm lying to everyone," he said.

"I'm sorry baby I didn't mean it like that," she said apologizing.

"I know this shit just crazy as fuck," he said.

"I agree but we in it now so let me know what you wanna do tonight and I'm gonna see if I can get out," she said.

"Ok baby," Peanut said as he hung up. He went to his contacts and dialed Baby. She didn't answer. He sat the phone in the seat and turned up the music as he rode home.

Mali walked in the house and seen Tina messing with her phone. He closed the door and walked over to the couch. "Hey, baby," he said as he leaned in to kiss her. He looked at her as she pecked his lips then went back to her phone. "Well it's good to see you too he said irritated, my day was great," He turned and walked to the kitchen as she got up from the couch.

"I'm sorry baby, I was talking to Onika. She wants me to step out with her tonight if that's ok with you?" she said.

Mali was relieved he didn't have to come up with an excuse. "That's fine, Tina, where y'all going?"

"Just a bar to do a little dancing," she said shaking her ass.

He slapped it as he headed to the bedroom. She followed behind him. "So, what you gonna do tonight talk to your *little* girlfriend's on Facebook?"

"I told you I ain't talking to no chicks," he got irritated. "When you gonna let this shit go cause I'm not fucking anyone else," he screamed.

She pushed his face. "Mali you may not be fucking anyone, but someone has your mind and thoughts other than me and I'm not stupid so tell me the truth," she sat on the bed and looked at him.

"The truth is I'm tired, I had a long day, and I just wanna relax," he said.

He turned and walked towards the bathroom. He stopped and turned to her. "You know if you were doing what you were supposed to do around here you wouldn't be so insecure about yourself," he yelled as he closed the door and left her with her thoughts.

Tina got up and went to her closet. *Why did I marry that asshole?* She picked up a white dress and some red heels. She grabbed the essentials needed to put her outfit on point. As she walked back into the room, she noticed Mali's phone on the bed.

"Oh, he slipping," she said as she picked up his phone. She saw a notification from My Little Secret. "Who the hell is *My Little Secret?*" She tapped the message, but the phone wouldn't unlock, and she had locked it before for guessing too many times. She put down his phone and went to get dressed.

"You sexy bitch," she said as she stood in the mirror loving her look for the night. She came out of the bathroom and walked back into the room and noticed Mali was still in the damn bathroom, so she grabbed her keys and headed out the door.

After she took out her phone to text Onika and let her know she was on her way, she stood in the driveway looking at the whips. "I'm feeling luxurious and beautiful tonight, so I'll drive the Range Rover since it's springtime." She hopped in and started up the truck. Making sure her Bluetooth was on, she pulled out the driveway heading to the club. She texted Peanut and told him she was out.

Peanut felt his phone vibrate as he walked into the house. "Baby, where the hell you at?" He yelled as he dialed her again but still no answer. He looked at his text message from Tina. He replied.

I'm about to shower and I'll hit you.

He sat the phone down and went to the shower.

Andrea looked at her phone and ignored the call.

"Girl, who you keep ignoring," Ashley said as she pulled into the club parking lot.

"Qwan's ass girl, Andrea said putting on her makeup, he didn't respond to me so I'm not answering him."

"You childish," Ashley said laughing.

"I have been good for way too long without a ring. I'm having no drama fun tonight," Andrea said. They got out of the truck and went inside the club. Andrea pulled out her phone and text Mali:

Hey baby, I snuck out and I'm ready for you so call me.

She put her phone in her purse and went to the bar. She ordered a drink then went and sat down. She looked at Tina as she walked into the club. "Damn she sexy as fuck," she said to herself.

"Who you looking at?" Ashley said as she turned around. "Oh, I see you on that *I think I want a woman shit again,* knowing you ain't gonna do shit," she said as she sipped her drink.

"You stupid, that bitch just sexy as fuck," Andrea said laughing. "She ok," Ashley said.

"I'll be back girl I'm gonna go buy her a drink," Andrea said.

"Oh, so we balling and buying drinks. Oh yeah, we balling now?" Ashley said.

"No silly, baby gave me some money today," Andrea said smiling.

"Girl, I know Qwan cheap ass ain't gave you no money so is there something you wanna tell me, Andrea?"

She gave her a stare but didn't get an answer. "Whatever go buy ya drink," she laughed as she took another sip.

Andrea walked to the bar and touched Tina's back as she sat by her. Her skin was soft. "Excuse me, I'm Andrea and you're sexy as fuck. Can I buy you a drink?"

"Wow, you got more balls than half the men in here. Hello, I'm Tina and I'll take a Tequila Sunrise."

"Hey, make it two," Andrea said handing the bartender a twenty. She kept looking at Tina. "I'm not that bold sweetie, I have never been with a woman, but I do wonder."

"Really? Well, let's get the nerves out the way." Tina leaned in and kissed Andrea deeply. She pulled her body off the stool and pulled her close as their kiss intensified. She finally released her. They both just looked at each other until the bartender interrupted their thoughts.

"Come sit with us," Andrea said. She grabbed her drink and Tina's hand as she led them back to the table.

"This is my friend Ashley, Ashley this is Tina."

"Hey girl, Ashley said, you working that dress."

"Thanks, girl, Tina said, I wanted to feel pretty."

"And you did that," Andrea said rubbing her leg.

"Oooohhhh on that note I'm going to find some dick," Ashley said. She got up from the table and went to the dance floor.

Andrea looked at Tina. "Listen I have never in my life felt an attraction like this for a woman but just sitting beside you has my nipples hard and my pussy wet," Tina reached and slid her hand between Andrea's thighs. She rubbed her pussy and felt the wetness through the thong.

"Yeah that pussy wet as hell," she said pulling her hand back. She licked her fingers slowly. "So, you ready to get out of here?"

Andrea looked at her eyes hard. "Fuck yeah, just let me go tell my homegirl I'm about to leave."

"Okay," Tina said slapping her ass as she got up from the table. She watched as Andrea walked on the dance floor to talk to Ashley. She checked her phone and read the message from Peanut. She put it back in her purse and grabbed her keys as Andrea walked back up.

"You ready?" Andrea asked as she leaned in and kissed Tina on the neck.

"Yes," she said in a soft voice. They both walked towards the door and went to the parking lot. "I'm in that Range Rover over there, the black one," Tina said pointing.

"Damn, baby, I see you have really good taste," Andrea said. She opened the door and got in as Tina got in the driver's seat.

"So, where are we going?" Tina said looking at Andrea. She leaned over and put her tongue on Andrea's lips and licked them slowly before going into her mouth. Andrea moaned at the feeling of a woman's tongue inside her mouth then she giggled like a kid.

"You ok," Tina asked laughing. "I think I hit a hot spot."

"Oh, I think you gonna hit a lot of my hot spots tonight," Andrea said smiling. "What's up, I got half on a room."

"No little sexy," Tina said putting her hand on her leg. "You bought me a drink, I got the room." She started the car and drove to the hotel. The spring weather felt good as they rode with the windows down. They made it to the hotel and parked by the door.

"I'm gonna go in here and get this room, you chilling?" Tina asked opening the door.

"I'm coming there's no need to waste any time," she said as she opened the door. She grabbed Tina's hand as they walked into the hotel.

After paying they both went looking for room 109. Once she found it, Andrea turned Tina around and pushed her against the door. She kissed her deeply as Tina moaned. Andrea put her hand under her sundress and felt no panties. She spread her legs and played with her pussy while kissing her neck, using her other hand to pinch her nipples.

"Damn!" Someone said from down the hall. Andrea caught herself and grabbed the room key from Tina. She opened the door and they entered the darkness of the room.

Andrea instantly started to undress and Tina followed suit. She crawled on the bed as Tina grabbed her ass spreading her cheeks and licking her from her pussy to her ass while she moaned with pleasure as she reached back and pulled Tina deeper eating her pussy from the back. She used her tongue to explore all of Andrea.

"Your pussy tastes good," Tina said.

She put her fingers inside Andrea moving them in a slow-motion as she licked her asshole.

"OH MY GOD!" Andrea screamed as she squirted all over Tina's face.

Tina kept her mouth sliding on her clit as the juices hit her face loving the taste of Andrea. She moved her tongue around her pussy until she felt the juices flowing again. Andrea screamed and moved her hips as Tina played with her pussy.

"Damn Tina, you got me cumming all over this bed. Let me see what I can do to you," Andrea said sitting up.

Tina smiled as Andrea opened her legs crawling between them kissing her body while pushing her down on the bed. She licked her nipples as she stroked her pussy in a steady motion. Tina moaned as her body felt the erratic pressure cumming out.

Andrea moved to her neck kissing it as she pulled her body close. She felt so many emotions as her body touched Tina, their pussies rubbing with wetness dripping.

Andrea got up and laid on her back.

"Come sit on my face," she said to Tina grabbing her cheek.

"Oh yeah? I hope you ready for this." Tina said standing up.

She moved her body down until she felt Andrea release the deep breath she was holding. When she felt her tongue inside her pussy, she moaned loudly with a healthy voice. Andrea grabbed her ass and pulled her pussy close so she could work her clit.

Tina allowed her to freestyle enjoying the feeling of a woman's touch. She reached back and pressed Andrea's hands to the bed as she opened her legs and spread her pussy across her face.

Tina moved in a motion that sounded like a beat as she humped her hips up and down on Andrea's mouth creaming all over her face. Screaming and shaking she came like never before. Her body fell on Andrea as she grabbed her thighs instantly pushing her legs back and taking her into her mouth eating her pussy upside down making her fuck every inch of her face until she squirted so hard that her juices hit the wall.

Andrea screamed as she came in a way she never had. She sat up and looked at her nut on the wall and they both started laughing.

"Baby, I haven't come like that in a minute, hell, probably ever. You got some skills I see," Andrea said.

She kissed Tina before she laid on her chest.

"So, do you, sweetie, Tina said still shaking from Andrea's tongue, give me a few and we can have a round two."

"Baby you can have as many rounds as you want," Andrea said smiling.

e Photography OKC

3

Summer

"Hot girl Summer…" Andrea sang as she walked through the house into the kitchen. She grabbed the coffee pot and went to the sink still dancing as she made the coffee. Qwan came around the corner and grabbed her waist. She started grinding on him as they both started moving their bodies to the beat. She turned her body and hugged him. He lifted her as she wrapped her legs around his waist.

"Well good morning baby, you're normally gone by the time I get up," she said kissing his lips.

"Yeah, I am but I needed to do something this morning before I left," Qwan said.

"He lifted her shirt and grabbed her breasts squeezing them as she started to moan.

"Damn baby, what is it you need?" she said whispering in his ear.

"You," he said as he sat her on the kitchen counter. He squatted down and put her legs on his shoulders as he pulled her pussy closer to his mouth. He went in fast putting her clit in his mouth sucking it till the juices came like a Capri Sun.

Andrea pushed his head down as his tongue slid inside her pussy. She moved her hips slowly as the music played, moaning and cumming as she rode his face on the now wet counter.

She grabbed his ears and pulled him up. He gave her a look as she pushed him back and jumped off the counter. She walked up to him reaching her arms until she touched his chest. She started kissing his nipples slowly using her tongue to excite him. Every time she stroked her tongue, she felt his dick jump through his boxers, so she reached down and pulled it out through the hole stroking him slowly.

He grabbed her ass before she went down. She licked it from the tip to the boxers all the way around until she got back to the head. Playing with it she used her tongue to tease and please him. She felt him get hard and jump as she bounced his dick on her tongue. Holding his tip in her mouth as she pulled down his boxers. She let him go as the boxers went past her lips.

When his dick jumped back up, she caught it and started sucking it slowly. Grabbing it with her hand she stroked him as she slowly made his dick wet. She looked up at him to see his face, but it was lost.

She took him out of her mouth then started sucking him deeper and deeper until all of him was hitting the back of her throat.

She gripped his ass and started moving his hips so that his dick could fuck her throat. He grabbed the back of her head as he stroked in and out of her mouth feeling all of her tongue and throat.

"Fuck girl, gon' let me fuck that face then." he said.

He was enjoying himself so she continued to take him in as deep as he could get until he pulled out, reached down and picked her up by her ass and lifted her until they were face to face. He kissed her as she positioned his dick inside her pussy then slowly slid her down as she moaned kissing his ear.

"Oh Baby!" she screamed as he hit her spots with every stroke. She felt him when he came inside her as she looked at his face noticing his eyes were still closed. She kissed him passionately before getting off of him.

"Thank you for pleasing me this morning baby I needed that." she said as she kissed him again.

"Already. I gotta get ready," he said as he walked to the bathroom and closed the door.

"Oh well," she said going back to her coffee. After making her cup she went back to the room. She picked up her phone and seen she had a text from Mali.

Mali: GM Babe

Andrea: Good morning cutie. Wyd

Mali: Just got out the shower, about to hit the streets. You trying to meet up today? It's hot outside today too.

Andrea: Really? You ain't trying to see me. I been patient and waiting for your dick since last Winter. And yeah, it's hot outside, what that mean?

Mali: LMAO. I see you in a mood this morning. That means to put on a nice tight sundress and come meet me at the hotel.

Andrea: Oh yeah? You ain't playing huh? When and where?

Mali: Days Inn downtown. Room 319. I'll be there laying in the bed. 2:00.

Andrea: Ok

Andrea jumped across the bed and went to her closet and found a dress she hadn't had an opportunity to wear yet, so she took it out and laid it on the bed. She went to her shoe closet and picked out a pair of heels. When she came out of the closet, Qwan was standing by the bed.

"And where you think you going in this dress, on the couch?" Qwan said holding up the dress.

"Whatever, Qwan, I wanna feel sexy today," she said taking the dress from him.

"You can feel sexy sitting on the couch," he said pointing.

"I'm going with my girls," she said.

"Naw you ain't, you gonna stay at this house and clean then cook my dinner," Qwan said with a pissed off look on his face.

"Excuse me who do you think you talking to?" She said rolling her eyes.

"What you mean?" He said standing up.

"Nigga, I'm grown, and you don't own me," she said walking towards the bathroom.

"You think I'm playing like I won't punish that ass!" He said slapping her ass.

"Your dick gotta get bigger for that," she said as she closed the door.

She started the shower then sat on the toilet.

I guess today is the day, she thought as she flushed and got in the shower.

Qwan laughed as he got dressed. He pulled out his phone and sent a text.

Qwan: What up Ma

Side: Hey sexy. What's up

Qwan: I'm trying to feel that pussy today. You trying to link up for a few?

Side: Yeah but I don't want no cheap-ass room this time. I'm worth more than $32.

Qwan: Here you go. Aight, meet me at Days Inn downtown. I will text you the room number.

Side: Ok

Qwan put his phone down and got dressed. He grabbed his keys and left before Andrea got out of the shower. After checking his balance, he pulled off.

Andrea came out of the bathroom glad she was alone. She put on her dress and heels then stood in the mirror looking at how sexy she looked before picking up her phone and dialing Tina.

Tina: Hey you, what you doing on this beautiful day?

Andrea: Finally, about to get some side dick. I'm about to go meet him in a few.

Tina: Oh yeah, you mean the one you been talking to for months? Who is he girl?

Andrea: Yes, him and he is who he is that's all I'm saying until I find out how good the dick is.

Tina: Girl you silly, well I'm about to meet my side piece as well today but he's one I can't talk about cause I ain't supposed to be fucking him.

Andrea: Say what? Now you've been keeping secrets you can't tell me.

Tina: I ain't telling shit.

Andrea: Ok so you wanna grab a drink tonight?

Tina: Sure girl, I'll call you tonight.

Andrea: Ok

They hung up as Andrea grabbed her keys and looked at the time as she walked out the door and got in her car. After setting her music she drove off and headed to the hotel.

Mali got to the room early to set the mood. He lit candles and put them around the hot tub as he started the water. He went to the bathroom and got the bubbles he bought then put them in the tub. He went and sat on the bed.

Before he could grab the remote, he heard a knock at the door. When he opened it, his

43

smile widened as Andrea stood there in a Gold sundress with the shoes to match, set off because her nails and toes matched as well.

He took her by the hand and led her into the room. He just stood and looked at her until she broke his daydream.

"Umm...Baby, you gonna turn off that water or you trying to make a pool?" She said pointing at the hot tub.

"My bad, your beauty sent me to another world," he said as he turned off the water. She laughed as she sat her purse on the table, walked up to him and wrapped her arms around his neck and kissed his lips.

"Thank you for all of this it's really sweet of you," she said as she kissed him again.

"Well I had you wait so long that I wanted it to be special, so I did a little extra," he said picking her up sitting her on the bed.

Reaching down he took off her shoes and rubbed her feet. He stood her up and slid her dress off and watched as it fell to the floor.

"Amazing. No panties," he said.

She smiled as he reached back with his right hand, unstrapping her bra and kissing her nipple. Feeling her take a deep breath, he grabbed her hand and led her to the hot tub. Her body got excited as she stepped in the water. No man had done this much for her in a long time. She smiled sitting in the water feeling the bubbles tickle her pussy as they covered her body. She looked up and seen Mali undressing.

"Take it off Baby," she said in a horny voice.

Mali slowly took off his shirt shaking his pecks as he threw the shirt on the floor. Loving the look she had on her face he loosened his pants and let them fall to the floor.

"Oh, I see you didn't wear underwear either," she said.

He laughed as he got in the hot tub positioning his body so that she could relax between his legs. She laid back on him and took a deep breath as he put his arms around her body. She grabbed the remote and turned on the TV as Mali reached for a towel.

He started washing her body as she tried to cuddle closer. Moving his hand, she turned her body around and sat on his lap. Kissing him passionately while rubbing his chest and squeezing his nipples.

"I see you ready for real," he said picking her up out of the tub. He kissed her to the bed. He laid her on her back kissing her nipples softly as he continued his way down and as he licked the outside of her pussy she began to squirm on the bed.

"Oh no you don't!" he said pulling her back to his mouth. He put his tongue deep in her instantly tasting her insides. She moaned as he continued to lick and stroke her pussy with his tongue pushing her legs up licking her asshole in circles.

"Damn baby that shit feels so fucking good. Oh shit, please don't stop!" she yelled.

He kept going as he slid his finger inside her pussy. She started to feel it as she humped his tongue and fucked his finger. When she came it was like an explosion in a water factory with juices going everywhere wetting the bed even more. Mali stood up and turned around to grab a towel. She looked at his ass and her mouth watered. She jumped up and grabbed his arms pushing him on the bed.

"Damn baby," he said as he tried to sit up, but she pushed him back down.

"Lay on your stomach," she said as she rolled him over.

"On my stomach, why?" he said.

"Because I wanna do something different." She licked his ass cheek.

"Hold on now ma, I don't play that ass shit." He said crawling away giving her a look.

"Listen, I'm the type of woman that pleases in every way even when you think it's uncomfortable," she said pulling him back.

"Ain't no pleasure in my ass baby none whatsoever," he said.

Rubbing his cheeks, she said, "Oh, there's some pleasure it just takes a woman like me to show you, so relax and let me do what I do," she started kissing his back.

"I don't think you should do that," he said.

"Why not?" she asked.

47

"What's the point? he said.

"Hitting that G-Spot, it's an amazing feeling baby," she said as she cuffed his ass.

"Men ain't got no G-Spot," he said laughing.

"You wanna bet?" she asked laughing.

"Bet what?" he said.

"Oh, my hair going to need done after this session," she said.

"Listen, it ain't no way that shit gonna," he started. But before he could finish his sentence, she had her tongue on his asshole.

"Oh damn," he said as he put his head on the bed. "Damn." She continued to lick his asshole while pleasuring his cheeks with her hands. She could tell he was nervous, so she slowed down and spread his cheeks then stuck her tongue inside his ass hitting his G-Spot. He moaned with pleasure as she swirled her tongue around.

She looked down and seen his dick jump and get rock hard, so she turned him over then reached and grabbed a condom off the dresser. She opened it and put it in her mouth as she slid it on his dick.

"Damn, I didn't know you were this freaky," he said as he grabbed her head.

She moved his hands and crawled on top of his body putting his dick inside her as she took a deep breath. Once he was as deep as he could go, she started bouncing on him slowly trying to slide the rest of him in.

"Damn, baby, I didn't know this dick was this big," she said moaning and screaming as he sped up his strokes going deeper inside her. She screamed and rode his dick like a champ, matching his strokes beat for beat.

After she came a few times he picked her up and laid her on the bed as he continued to stroke. She moaned as she wrapped her legs around his back and let him dig deep inside her feeling every inch of him with every stroke.

When she heard him moan with pleasure, she knew he was about to cum, so she pulled him down and pressed his body to hers. When he came he was deep inside her. She felt his dick jump as the nut came out of him. She looked at him and smiled.

"You look tired but damn that dick was good," she said.

"Oh, it ain't over cause we not done yet," he said reaching for another condom.

He turned her around and bent her over on the bed spreading her pussy lips and pushed his dick inside.

"Oh shit, slow down," she said lunging forward.

"Girl you better take this dick!" He said.

He put it back in and stroked her pussy making wetness fly every time he went deep. He was going so fast that his balls hit her clit with every stroke. She just kept moaning and cumming as he gave her pleasure that she hasn't felt in so long screaming as she bounced her ass back. When he finally came again it felt amazing.

They both fell on the bed and stared at the ceiling. Mali grabbed her hand and played with her fingers as his phone went off. He reached for it and seen it was Peanut texting him. He ignored it and looked at the time.

"Damn, time flew by quick," he said.

"It be like that when you go to a different world. She said sitting up. What time is it anyway?"

"4:15. Guess we need to make a move huh," he said sitting up as well.

"I guess so but how about a quickie before we go?" she said rubbing his dick.

She looked at him with wanting eyes as she jacked him off. He laid her down and kissed her neck as she put him inside her. When he fell inside her, the bare sensation made her moan long and loud as he looked at her face while he dug deep feeling her wetness gush inside her.

He loved the look on her face as she grabbed his back and pulled him close as he moved his hips. He sped up his stroke as he felt the explosion cumming, so he pulled out just in time for his nut to hit her stomach. Laughing, she got up and went to the bathroom and started the shower before coming back into the room. She grabbed his hand and they both went to shower.

Qwan pulled over at the hotel before he reached for his phone and sent a text. While waiting on a response he seen a familiar car parked in the parking lot.

I know that ain't Andrea's car. What the fuck is she doing here? He said looking closely at the car. He picked up his phone and called Andrea, but she didn't answer.

Her ass must have gone through my phone trying to catch me but not today, he said.

He sent Side a text to reschedule before he pulled out the parking lot.

4

Fall

Qwan sat in the living room flipping through the channels when he looked up and seen Andrea coming down the stairs.

"Good morning," he said.

"Good morning baby, she said as she kissed him on the cheek, you ok this morning?" she said kissing his cheek on her way to the kitchen.

"Yeah, I'm good, just thinking about today," he said. He walked in the kitchen to her holding a box.

"Happy birthday baby. Go ahead and open it," she said handing him the box. He opened the box and his eyes got wide when he saw the new Jordan's and Polo outfit to match.

"Damn thank you, girl. I really appreciate this," he said leaning in to kiss her. He went to the couch to try on the shoes as she followed. "These joints are nice." He said modeling.

"You deserve it I guess," she said.

"I do deserve it," he said returning her smile.

"So, we going out tonight?" she asked.

"Going out? I'm not really feeling no club," he said looking confused.

"You don't have a problem going out any other night," she said irritated.

"What you tripping for?" he said.

"You still don't want me to meet any of your friends like I'm ugly?" she said with an attitude.

"Yo chill with that bullshit, I'm gonna hit the homie and set up a dinner," he said grabbing his phone.

"I guess," she said walking in the other room. She slammed the door as Qwan unlocked his phone. He went to his text messages and sent Mali a text.

Qwan: What up Dogg

Mali: Qwan Peanut Taylor. Happy Birthday, Dogg. What you got up.

Qwan: Thanks, Bruh. Not shit trying to take one of my ladies out tonight. You and Tina wanna join us?

Mali: I'm wit it. Let me get with Tina. What time you trying to go?

Qwan: Shiiid around 7. At the Bar and Grill on the North.

Mali: Aight bet. See you then, Dogg.

Qwan put his phone down and walked to the bedroom. He opened the door to Andrea standing by the window.

"Yo we going to the bar and grill with my homie and his wife at seven so be ready," he said.

He closed the door and went back to the couch.

Mali went to ask Tina about tonight but when he walked into the room she was still in the bed. He walked over and touched her shoulder as she turned over.

"What time is it?" she said blocking the light in her face.

"It's 11:00," Mali said looking at his watch.

"Then why you waking me up so early?" she said.

"Peanut's birthday is today and we gonna double with him and his date at the bar and grill tonight."

"A date, oh he got a girl now?" she said looking irritated.

"I guess, why the hell you care?" Mali said looking confused.

"I don't, it's just a surprise that's all," she said getting out of bed.

"Whatever just be ready by seven," he said walking out closing the door.

Tina picked up her phone and text Peanut.

TINA: Oh, you got a bitch now?

She got no response, so she went and started the shower. "Gonna be a long day."

That night Mali and Tina made it to the bar first. Mali used valet to park as they walked in the bar.

"I'm gonna go wash my hands and I'll meet you at the table," he said.

Tina rolled her eyes and pulled out her phone. She noticed Andrea didn't hit her up today then remembered her dude birthday was today. She put the phone in her purse as the waiter escorted her to the table.

Andrea and Qwan pulled in but he parked his own car. They got out of the car and walked into the bar.

"I need to use the ladies room so I will meet you at the table," she said touching his arm.

She walked off as Qwan went to the table and seen Tina sitting alone. He touched her shoulder then leaned in and kissed her cheek.

"Hey sexy," he said sitting down.

"Hey Peanut, where's your date?" Tina said with an attitude.

"I know you not jealous like you not here with your husband," Peanut said laughing.

"Your point?" Tina said.

"Then you better stop acting," Peanut said.

"Not even acting baby, I just don't like being lied to," she said rolling her eyes.

"I didn't lie, you know I fuck other bitches," Peanut said.

"So, this is not your girl? Tina asked.

"This just one I'm fucking for my birthday," he said smiling.

"Whatever," she said.

"Now chill, Mali coming." he said sitting back.

Mali walked up to the bar to order drinks before he went to the table.

"What up Dogg, Happy Birthday again," Mali said as they showed love.

"Thanks, Dogg," Peanut said.

"I ordered us a bottle of Crown. Where's ya date?" Mali said.

"Awe she went to the bathroom she should be out in a minute," Peanut said.

"So, who is this girl, Dogg, cause you don't usually bring any around," Mali asked.

The waitress walked over and set glasses on the table along with a bottle of Crown.

"Just a lil tender, nobody important," Peanut said smiling at Tina.

Andrea came out of the bathroom and walked towards the table. When she got close, she saw Tina sitting at the table with Qwan.

"What the Fuck," she said as she got closer. When Qwan saw her, he stood up.

"There she is now," Peanut said pointing at her.

Tina saw her first and took a deep breath with a look on her face that would stop a bullet.

"Well hello, I'm Tina and you are?" Tina said standing up.

"I'm Andrea," she said touching her hand.

Chills went through her body feeling Tina's skin in her hand again. When Mali heard the name Andrea, he almost choked on his drink.

Man, I got to be tripping, he said to himself as he turned around. When he saw Andrea, his heart stopped. She looked at him and instantly put her head down.

"Come on and sit down, baby," Peanut said pulling out her chair.

She sat down slowly before she looked up and everyone had a blank look on their face until Tina broke the silence.

"So how long have you been messing with Peanut?" Tina asked leaning on the table.

"Yo, it's my BIRTHDAY so what's up with the Q&A?" Peanut said standing up.

"We just making conversation," Tina said smiling.

"Conversation huh?" Peanut said.

"I mean you just popped out of nowhere with her, so I'm intrigued," Tina said.

"We've been together for almost three years," Andrea said attempting to calm the conversation.

"Three years? Mali said confused.

"Peanut," Tina said looking at him

"Dogg, come holla at me," Mali said. He got up and walked to the bar but Peanut sat there for a second. He finally got up and went to the bar.

Once they were alone Tina leaned on the table. "So, Andrea this is the man you been with all this time?" Tina asked.

"Yes, but you know what's funny?" Andrea said looking into Tina's eyes.

"What's that baby?" Tina said sipping her drink.

"The guy you are with is the guy I met on Messenger," Andrea said.

"You mean the one who made you hot as the summertime temp?" Tina asked.

"The one I fucked for hours then sat on the phone telling you about it," Andrea said.

Tina sat back in her seat trying to speak but was lost for words. She turned and looked at Mali making sure he was still at the bar before she spoke.

"Oh, so the guy I couldn't tell you about is my husband's best friend Peanut aka Qwan," Tina said.

"Wait, you mean my Qwan?" Andrea said holding up her hand.

"Your Qwan," Tina said.

They both started laughing as they picked up their drinks toasting.

"This is some crazy shit," Tina said.

"We may as well just put it out there since come to find out we all fucking each other anyway," Andrea said laughing.

Andrea was laughing as Mali and Peanut came back to the table. Peanut looked like he'd just got yelled at by his father. Andrea got up and looked at Tina.

"Let's get out of here," she said grabbing her purse. Tina got up and they both started walking towards the door. Mali looked at Peanut and threw up his hands. He put a hundred-dollar bill on the table and they both went outside.

Tina and Andrea were already in the car waiting. They both sat in the back seat so that the men could ride in the front. Peanut got in the car as Mali paid the valet.

"So, where are we going?" He asked once he got in the car.

"We are going to the house to have some drinks," Tina said looking out the window.

"Okay, cool," Mali said driving off.

He turned up the music as they cruised to the house in silence then parked in the driveway.

When they all got out and walked into the house, Tina and Andrea went to the kitchen to get glasses while Mali turned on the lights.

Peanut sat on the couch as Mali grabbed the remote and turned on the TV. The Laker game was on, so they sat back.

"Tina why are we at your house which is nice as fuck by the way," Andrea said.

"Because girl we gonna turn this into a swingers party," Tina smiled as she poured the crown.

"Girl what you talking about?" Andrea asked.

"Like I said we all already fucking so let's fuck plus I wanna taste you again," Tina said.

Andrea stood there rubbing her nipples as the thoughts went through her mind. Yes, she has watched this type of shit on X-videos but to physically be in the situation turned her on. She felt Tina touch her arm, so she opened her eyes.

"So how you wanna do this?" Andrea said smiling.

"Well, why don't we start the show off?" Tina said picking up the drinks.

Tina laughed as they walked back into the living room where Mali and Peanut were watching the game. She handed each of them a drink and gave Mali a look as he tried not to stare at Andrea.

"Y'all enjoying the game," she said sitting at the table with Andrea.

Before they could answer she pulled Andrea up and sat her on her lap looking at her deeply before their lips met. They kissed passionately as Tina started to move her hands to explore Andrea.

Peanut saw it first, so he tapped Mali on the leg and pointed. He tried to speak but was lost for words.

Mali got up and started to walk over but Tina pointed back to the couch, so he stepped back and sat down slowly.

Tina moved her hand back, sliding the straps down so that Andrea's breasts would show as she took one in her mouth and sucked the nipple slow while gripping her ass. She looked up at Andrea before she slapped her ass and told her to get on the table.

Andrea obeyed because obviously, Tina was in charge, so she stood up and slid her panties off before she laid on the kitchen table. Tina got up and took off her clothes as well. She leaned in and kissed Andrea before she started using her lips to explore her body.

She licked one long time from her nipples to her pussy. Raising her legs, she went in using her tongue to spin Andrea into an orgasm.

Mali watched in shock at what Tina and Andrea were doing. He turned to look at Peanut who was already undressing.

"Dogg, what the fuck you doing?" Mali said

"Nigga, do you see mine and yours on that table? Sit back and enjoy wit your scary ass," Peanut said taking off his pants.

Peanut was naked by that time. He stood up and walked to the end of the table so he could see better. As Andrea moaned from Tina's mouth, his dick jumped not knowing which one he wanted to fuck more.

Tina worked Andrea until she sat in her own juices. When she turned around Peanut was standing with his dick in his hand. She looked at Mali sitting on the couch still looking nervous, so she grabbed Andrea by the hand and helped her up.

"Why don't you go and help him relax?" Tina asked.

Tina slapped Andrea's ass walking towards Peanut and grabbing his dick pulling him to the couch.

When Mali tried to sit up Andrea jumped on his lap kissing him deeply as his hands grabbed her ass. She ripped off his shirt and unbuckled his pants.

"Take off these fucking clothes," she said pulling him up.

She grabbed his dick as he took off his pants. He sat back down as she got on her knees.

Tina laid Peanut on the couch before she sat on his face and started grinding and riding while rubbing her pussy all over his tongue. She stroked his dick as she fucked his face. She looked over at Andrea sucking Mali's dick with his eyes closed so Andrea knew what she was doing.

Tina leaned over and took Peanut in her mouth still riding his face as she played with the head so good, she felt him jump with every lick.

Andrea allowed Mali to have control putting his hand behind her head and slowly pushed his dick in and out of her wet ass mouth. He closed his eyes as he leaned his head back with passion running through him.

Peanut had no control over Tina as she humped his face. The pleasure she felt from his tongue sent chills threw her body as she creamed all over his face.

She turned her body around and sat on his dick. Peanut moaned aloud at the feeling of sliding in her without a condom as her wetness made his dick jump every time she made a move. Riding him, she grabbed his head and kissed him when she heard Andrea moaning so she turned to look.

Mali had Andrea laid across the loveseat with her legs in the air and his face between her legs with his tongue deep in her once again.

Andrea moaned as she moved her pussy around his face cummimg hard holding his head so he could catch every drop.

Mali tried to get up, but she pulled him close as she grabbed his dick and pushed him inside her.

"Oh Fuck!" He screamed.

He slid in and out of Andrea pleasing her with every stroke.

Peanut felt the nut cumming and tried to hold it, but Tina felt it too, so she sped up her pace pushing her weight on his chest with every bounce.

Andrea wrapped her legs around Mali and pushed him deeper allowing him access deep in her walls as she screamed with every stroke until she felt it.

Tina knew it was coming and wanted to feel it inside her, so she pushed him deep shaking her ass on his lap as she started grinding until she felt him explode inside her.

She screamed loud as Andrea moaned.

Mali tried to pull out, but her legs had him stuck, so he kept stroking trying to hold his nut in, but Andrea squeezed her pussy tight on his dick and his next stroke sent a hot sensation through her body. She grabbed Mali still shaking from cumming. Mali fell back on the couch as Tina got up and walked over to Andrea.

"Now this is a lot better don't you think so," Tina said sitting beside Andrea touching her face.

"Where the fuck all this come from?" Mali asked still confused.

"How we go from a birthday to a swinger party," Peanut said.

"Because we all fucking each other anyway," Andrea said.

"What you mean we all fucking?" Mali said standing up.

"Let's not play innocent Mali I fucked you last summer, very great dick by the way." Andrea said laughing.

"Oh, this shit funny." Peanut said.

"And I fucked Tina last Spring," she kissed Tina on the leg.

"And I been fucking Peanut every other week since last Winter," she looked at Andrea.

"Damn that long?" Andrea said.

"Sorry baby, I didn't know he was yours," Tina said looking at Andrea.

Mali looked at his homie with an angry face.

"Dogg, you been fucking my wife for almost a year?" he said standing up.

Tina did also and walked up to him.

"Now, Mali, we not gonna do that," she said touching his chest.

"Move Tina," Mali said.

"Listen, yes we all fucked up and apparently fucked each other but whatever cause now it's out," Tina said.

"I get it," Mali said shaking his homie hand.

"Dogg, I wanted to tell you." Peanut said.

"Whatever this shit was HOTT as fuck. Watching you fuck him had me excited and made me fuck her harder."

Tina smiled, "Well, that's a conversation for the morning." She looked at Peanut then back to Mali. "So y'all ready for *Round II*….??"

Made in the USA
Columbia, SC
28 September 2020

21481386R00045